Illustrated by the Disney Storybook Artists
Story adapted by Amy Adair

© Disney Enterprises, Inc.

Published by
Louis Weber, C.E.O.
Publications International, Ltd.
7373 North Cicero Avenue
Lincolnwood, Illinois 60712

www.pilbooks.com

Manufactured in China.

8 7 6 5 4 3 2 1

ISBN: 0-7853-9773-6

The whole kingdom was excited. King Triton's youngest daughter, Ariel, was going to make her singing debut.

"This will be the finest concert I've ever conducted," Sebastian the crab told the sea king. "Your daughters will be spectacular, especially little Ariel."

Sebastian took a deep breath. Then he tapped his conductor stick, and the concert began. All of the sea king's daughters emerged from giant oyster shells and sang.

But when it was Ariel's turn, there was silence.

"Ariel!" King Triton yelled.

Ariel was exploring a sunken ship with her friend Flounder.

"What do you think this is?" Ariel asked, picking up a fork. "Have you ever seen anything so wonderful?"

She was sure her friend Scuttle would know what it was. He lived above the sea and seemed to know all about the wonderful world of humans. Ariel and Flounder swam to the surface.

"This is very unusual," Scuttle said as he examined the fork. "It's a dinglehopper. Humans use this to straighten their hair."

Suddenly Ariel remembered the concert. She knew her father would be very upset.

Ariel raced back to the palace. She apologized to her
father and Sebastian for missing the concert.

Flounder tried to help Ariel. He began to tell Sebastian
and King Triton about their adventure. Then Flounder
accidentally told them about Scuttle.

King Triton knew Scuttle was a seagull. "You went up
to the surface!" King Triton roared. "You could have been
seen by humans. I never want to hear about you going to
the surface ever again!"

Ariel started to cry as she swam away.

King Triton told Sebastian to watch Ariel. He was to make sure that she did not get into any more trouble. Sebastian followed Ariel into her secret cave. The cave was filled with all kinds of gadgets and gizmos. Sebastian had never seen so many things from the world above the sea.

Ariel stared at her collection. More than anything she wanted to be with humans. She wished she could be part of their world.

Suddenly, Ariel
looked up and saw the
bottom of a ship. She swam
to the surface and saw that the
men on the ship were in the middle of a huge celebration.

Ariel wanted to get a closer look. She quietly climbed
up on the ship and peeked through a window. She watched
as the men danced, sang, and laughed. A friendly dog
spotted her. He wagged his tail and licked her face.

"Max!" Prince Eric yelled at the dog. Ariel stared at
Prince Eric. She had never seen a human so handsome.

Scuttle was flying over the sea when he spotted Ariel.
"Hello there, sweetie," Scuttle said, peering into the window.

"I have never seen humans this close before," Ariel whispered to Scuttle.

Ariel and Scuttle kept watching as a man named Grimsby unveiled a gigantic statue of Prince Eric. "Happy birthday, Eric," Grimsby said. "I had hoped this would be a wedding present for you."

Eric laughed. "The right girl is out there somewhere," Eric said, gazing into the sea. "I just haven't found her yet."

"A hurricane is coming!" a man suddenly yelled.

All the sailors ran to secure the ship's rigging. The ship rocked back and forth. Eric grabbed the ship's wheel and tried to hold it steady. It was no use. The men knew the ship was going to sink. All the sailors jumped safely into the lifeboats.

Woof! Max was still onboard! Eric quickly jumped into the raging sea and swam back to the sinking ship. He grabbed Max and put him in a lifeboat, but Eric sank to the bottom of the sea.

Ariel watched in horror as Eric sank deeper and deeper. She dove down after him and pulled him to the shore.

"He's so beautiful," Ariel told Scuttle. "I wish I could stay here beside him."

Ariel sang and talked to Eric until he started to wake up. Then she dashed back into the sea.

Everyone in the kingdom knew Ariel was in love.

"He loves me," Ariel said, picking a petal off a sea flower. "He loves me not. He loves me! I knew it!"

Sebastian shook his head. "Stop talking crazy," he said to Ariel.

"I have to see him again!" Ariel said. "I will swim up to his castle, then Flounder will splash around and get his attention."

The sea king was very happy to hear that Ariel was in love. But he thought she was in love with a merman. The sea king was furious when Sebastian told him Ariel was in love with a human.

King Triton found Ariel in her secret cave admiring the statue of Prince Eric that Flounder had found for her.

"I forbade you to have any contact with the human world," King Triton said.

"You don't even know him," Ariel cried.

"Humans are dangerous," King Triton said.

"Daddy," Ariel cried, "I love him."

King Triton did not know what else to do. He destroyed all of Ariel's treasures. Then he destroyed the statue of Prince Eric.

King Triton had banished Ursula, the sea witch, from the kingdom. She wanted revenge. She knew Ariel was the key to the sea king's undoing. So she sent her eels, Flotsam and Jetsam, to find Ariel.

"The sea witch can make all of your dreams come true," Flotsam hissed to Ariel.

"Just imagine you and the prince together forever," Jetsam said.

Ariel was scared. But she followed the eels to Ursula's cave. Ursula stirred a magic potion. She explained that the potion would turn Ariel into a human for three days. By the third day, Prince Eric had to kiss her. If he kissed her, she'd remain a human forever. But if he didn't, then Ariel would turn back into a mermaid and be Ursula's prisoner.

"Nothing is free," Ursula said. "So I'd like your voice."

Ariel thought for a moment, then agreed. As Ariel sang, Ursula captured her voice in a magic seashell.

Then Ariel's tail disappeared and in its place were legs. She kicked her legs, but she didn't know how to swim without a tail. Sebastian and Flounder grabbed her and swam to the surface.

Ariel examined her legs in awe. She wiggled her toes, then tried to stand up. Her legs were very wobbly. She fell back into the water.

"There's still time," Sebastian said. "We could go back and tell Ursula it was all a big mistake. Then you could go home…" Sebastian's voice trailed off.

Ariel looked at Sebastian sadly.

"You'd be just miserable for the rest of your life," Sebastian sighed. "I'll help you find your prince."

It wasn't long before Prince Eric and Max strolled
down the beach. Prince Eric was sure he recognized Ariel.
He thought she was the one he had been looking for.

"Have we met?" he asked her.

Ariel nodded her head.

"You can't speak," Prince Eric said, disappointed. "Then
you couldn't be who I thought you were."

Prince Eric took Ariel back to his palace. His servants
gave Ariel a beautiful pink ball gown to wear to dinner.
Prince Eric had never seen a prettier girl.

The next day, Prince Eric gave Ariel a tour of the entire kingdom. They set off in a horse-drawn carriage.

Flounder and Scuttle were sure Prince Eric was falling in love with Ariel. After a day of exploring the kingdom, Prince Eric and Ariel went on a romantic boat ride. They drifted through a beautiful lagoon.

Sebastian was getting nervous. He wanted to help Ariel, so he set the mood with a romantic tune.

Eric was falling in love with Ariel. He stared into her eyes. "I feel bad," he told her. "I don't even know your name. Is it Mildred?"

Ariel shook her head.

"How about Diana? Or Rachel?"

"It's Ariel," Sebastian whispered in Eric's ear.

"Ariel!" said Eric.

Ariel nodded happily.

"That's a pretty name," said Eric as he smiled.

Ursula watched Ariel and Prince Eric in her magic ball. She could see that Prince Eric was falling in love with Ariel. Things were not going as Ursula had planned. Just as Eric leaned in to kiss Ariel, the eels tipped the boat over.

"You did it!" Scuttle told Ariel in the morning. "Prince Eric is preparing to get married."

Ariel ran to find Eric. But he was standing next to another girl.

"Vanessa and I will be married at sunset," Eric told Grimsby. "Our wedding ship will leave at once."

Scuttle watched Vanessa admire herself in the mirror. But the reflection was Ursula's! The sea witch had tricked Eric. She had even used Ariel's voice.

Scuttle told Ariel everything that he had seen. Flounder helped Ariel swim to the ship where the wedding was going to be held.

Scuttle went to steal the seashell that Ursula had around her neck, but the shell fell and broke. It had Ariel's voice trapped inside. When Ariel got her voice back, she began to sing.

Eric then knew she was the girl he had been looking for. He leaned in to kiss Ariel just as the sun set.

But it was too late. Ariel had become a mermaid again.

King Triton could not break Ursula's spell, so he traded himself for Ariel's freedom. With King Triton's trident, Ursula became a gigantic and powerful ruler of the sea. Her head touched the clouds.

Eric knew he had to save Ariel. He sailed his boat right into Ursula, who sank to the very bottom of the ocean and disappeared forever.

With Ursula now gone, King Triton was free.

King Triton wanted his daughter to be happy. He knew Ariel and Eric truly loved each other, so he turned Ariel back into a human.

"I'm going to miss her so much," King Triton said.

Prince Eric had finally found his princess. He and Ariel were married soon after and lived a long and happy life together.